1

First Published 2021 by Yearn to Learn Children's Books

ISBN 978-0-9574392-4-5
Text Copyright © Chris Jones 2021
Illustrations Copyright © Becca Wain 2021

2

Dear Mums, Dads, Grandparents...

We really hope you love our book, and it helps your young mind(s) to see the value in themselves - that was always our aim!

If it's well-received, then we'd love to write and draw more. But getting seen as a newbie indie author is so hard! Your help would really be welcome. If you bought this on Amazon, please leave us a review - they mean the world to us. And if you're on Facebook, you can find our page- @yearntolearnbooks and discover our other books. A like would be great and a share amongst your friends would be awesome!

Thank you so much, Chris and Becca. x
yearntolearn.co.uk

Harley's not like other dogs,
she's called a basset hound.
Her butt goes left when she goes right,
with ears that sweep the ground.

Her walks are quite eventful,
often laughter turns to tears.
It's nice when grown-ups say, "how cute",
but kids - they swing her ears!

She loves it when its playtime,
games like hide 'n seek.

Until her shape spoils all
the fun.

It's then she feels a
freak.

6

Her legs are not the longest,
with centre of gravity low.
It often ends in drama,
and shouts of

"heave"

and "ho".

The greatest challenge is Lucy,
a yappy little chihuahua.
This tiny pooch, one third her size,
makes Harley shrink and cower.

She'd love to be like other dogs,

swimming lakes and catching balls.

Admired and feared by one and all

as the victor of
the brawls.

She'd been feeling flat for quite a while,
this fragile little pup.
But as her face is always sad,
no one knew what's up.

Then one night a man appeared,
on the talking box machine.
It was the most exciting thing,
she'd really ever seen.

He called himself a hypnotist,
was going to count to three.
Follow his instructions and

"be who you want to be".

She sat herself bolt upright,
and never made a sound.
A shiny thing swung to and fro.
She was totally spellbound.

His voice sunk to a whisper,
as he said to close her eyes.
When he counted three
    and clapped his hands,
a superstar would rise.

And as if by magic,
that's just how it went.
For the first time in
who knows how long,
Harley felt content.

15

She felt a great deal taller,

teeth larger than before.

With all this newfound confidence,

a lofty look she wore.

And on her next trip to the park
with faithful owner Nick.
She rampaged through
the undergrowth,

brought him back a giant stick.

A mate of hers called Mighty Mac,
was playing catch and fetch.
She used her super-canine powers,
and beat him at a stretch.

Then she saw her nemesis,
that pesky Mexican pest.
She threw her back a snarly glare,
no longer felt oppressed.

So when one day a fight broke out,
that'd normally have her retreating.
This time she jumped into the fray,
and dealt out quite a beating.

With all this sudden confidence,

she felt a new-born hound.

Now she could do anything,

the change was quite profound.

On a weekend family outing,
she swam a boggy mire.
But rather than impressing them,
it only drew their ire.

And when she next saw little Mac,

he cowered in trepidation.

Her oldest canine comrade,

had heard her reputation.

Even passing strangers,
no longer found her charming.
And kids had other ears to stroke,
it really was disarming.

Life as a super athlete,

was not quite as expected.

Instead of being popular,

she began to feel rejected.

Then one day in the garden,
came her reflection in the door.
Much to her amazement,
sat the same dog as before!

Had the powers gone away,

or were they just a trick?

Maybe they were never there,

or was she being thick?

Being like others did feel nice,

although it had been brief.

But seeing her old self once more,

just filled her with relief.

When mud was next an option,

she made a quick retreat.

Instead of getting shouted at,

she earned

a doggie

treat.

And on her next trip to the park,

she spied her buddy Mac.

She went down on her haunches,

to prove old Harley's back.

She'd learnt a powerful lesson.
In fact she felt quite blessed.
Being like others
            might sound fun...

but being herself was BEST!

We're on a mission to write 12 rhyming picture books in 12 months ...
and we'd love you to come on the journey with us!
Check out our other amazing books available now...

Princess Pea of Popty Ping

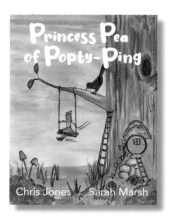

*Princess Penelope
is not like you and me.
She used to live in an old oak tree.
But then she uprooted,
which was a curious thing,
because now her address is Popty-Ping.*

Red Spotted Ned

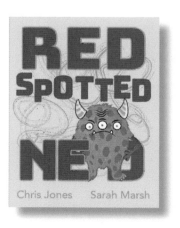

*On a little tiny lane,
in a tiny little town.
Lives an angry monster,
and he wears a GIANT frown!*

Myrtle the Hawksbill Turtle

Did you know there are only around 700
hawksbill turtles left on the planet?
This beautiful and heart-warming story
introduces the impact of climate change and
conservation, but in a gentle & upbeat way.

Here's some snippets...

On the shores of Costa Rica,
lives a gorgeous hawksbill turtle.
And if you've ever seen her,
you'll know her name is Myrtle.
Her shell is quite amazing,
its parts are called a scute.
A blend of awesome colours,
that make her look...a beaut!

Bessie Bibbs' Ginormous Fibs

The second book in our monster series.
This time we meet Bessie. She just can't help but
tell fibs. And whilst her intentions are good, they
keep getting her into trouble ... with very messy
consequences!

In the town of Biggle Wiggle,
lives the monster, Bessie Bibbs.
And all this lady wants to do,
is tell ginormous fibs!
The type of fibbers we might know,
tell stories wide and tall.
But Bessie's one of those you'd call,
a blessed know-it-all!

Visit us at yearntolearn.co.uk or search for our books on Amazon

Printed in Great Britain
by Amazon

33842534R00021